DISNEP
ALICE in WONDERLAND

Curiouser and Curiouser

Published by Creative Edge, LLC, 2009, an imprint of Dalmatian Press, LLC, Franklin, Tennessee 37067.
No part of this book may be reproduced or copied in any form without written permission from the copyright owner.

Printed in China

09 10 ZHE 10 9 8 7 6 5 4 3 2 1
CE12216 Disney 8x8 Storybook: Alice in Wonderland - Curiouser and Curiouser

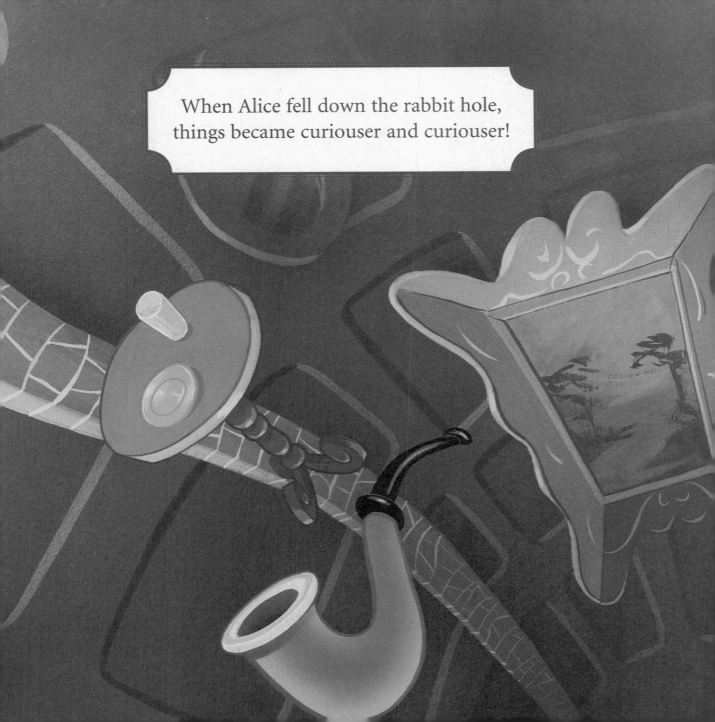

When Alice fell down the rabbit hole, things became curiouser and curiouser!

Most peculiar!
Odd creatures in a pool of tears!

Just a bit silly!
A Walrus and Carpenter coaxing oysters.

Very extraordinary!
A garden of talking flowers!

Strange, indeed!
Tea for three—served up with foolishness.

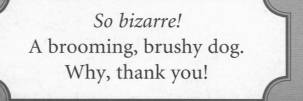

So bizarre!
A brooming, brushy dog.
Why, thank you!

Oh, wonderful!
A door with a talking Doorknob!
Will it take Alice home?

Or was it all just a wonder-filled dream?